The Chicken Salad

MARSHA DIANE ARNOLD • *pictures by* JULIE DOWNING

Dial Books for Young Readers • *New York*

Published by Dial Books for Young Readers
A member of Penguin Putnam Inc.
375 Hudson Street
New York, New York 10014

Designed by Ann Finnell
Printed in Hong Kong on acid-free paper
First Edition
1 3 5 7 9 10 8 6 4 2

Library of Congress Cataloging in Publication Data
Arnold, Marsha Diane.
The chicken salad club / by Marsha Diane Arnold ; pictures by Julie Downing.
p. cm.
Summary: Nathaniel's great-grandfather, who is 100 years old, loves
to tell stories from his past but seeks someone to join him
with a new batch of stories.
ISBN 0-8037-1915-9.—ISBN 0-8037-1916-7 (lib. bdg.)
[1. Old age—Fiction. 2. Great-grandfathers—Fiction.
3. Storytelling—Fiction.] I. Downing, Julie, ill. II. Title.
PZ7.A7363Ch1998 [Fic]—dc21 97-19375 CIP AC

*The illustrations were created with
watercolor and colored pencil on watercolor paper.*

For my grandmother
Myrtle Lippincott,
who told wonderful stories
for nearly a century

—M.D.A.

For Marilyn and Morris Sachs

—J.D.

Nathaniel Hopkins's great-grandfather was one hundred years old. His name was Henry Hopkins, but people called him Hank. Except for Nathaniel, who called him Greatpaw.

Every day after Nathaniel got home from school, he went next door to listen to Greatpaw's stories. Greatpaw made chicken salad sandwiches and Nathaniel poured lemonade.

When Greatpaw was settled in his chair and Nathaniel on the footstool, the storytelling began. "When I was a boy," Greatpaw said, "my brother and I made rafts of willow branches and sailed across the river to build hideouts."

"Tell me about the day of the storm," said Nathaniel.

"That day the river took us faster and farther than we'd ever been. We thought we'd never get back home."

Greatpaw chuckled. "When we did . . . we learned there was another purpose for willow branches."

After a sandwich Greatpaw continued. "When the Great War had come and gone, barnstormers flew their planes into town, puttin' on air shows."

"Upside down, like this," said Nathaniel, moving his hands in the air to demonstrate, the way he'd seen Greatpaw do so many times.

"Yes." Greatpaw smiled. "Rollin' in the sky. One fella walked on his plane's wings, hundreds of feet in the air. When I saw that, I began savin' my money to take flyin' lessons and buy a plane of my own."

Greatpaw paused, took a long swallow of lemonade, and told how he met Greatmaw at the Church Box Supper. "Her box was decorated with a model of a Curtiss Jenny. Course I had to buy it, even though the biddin' went a mite high.

"The next summer I took the money I'd saved for flyin' lessons and bought a farm instead. Greatmaw and I raised corn and hogs and five children."

Nathaniel looked at the faded picture of Greatmaw beside Greatpaw's chair. Greatpaw picked up the picture, rubbed the dust off it with his shirt sleeve, and softly said, "I miss her."

One afternoon after Nathaniel had poured lemonade, Greatpaw sat down in his chair and peered at Nathaniel over his spectacles. "Why, boy, I must have told you every story of my life well nigh a hundred times—as many times as I am years old. I've been thinkin' you need some new stories to be told."

"I like your stories, Greatpaw," Nathaniel answered.

Greatpaw rubbed his chin thoughtfully and said, "I know you do, but I need to hear a few new stories myself."

That was when Greatpaw had his idea for The Century Club.

Nathaniel helped Greatpaw post notices at the library and Patterson's Drugstore.

CALLING ALL CENTURY-OLD STORYTELLERS:
Get-acquainted meeting
Saturday noon
510 Piper Lane
To share Stories
Chicken Salad Sandwiches and Lemonade

A local TV reporter came to interview Greatpaw. Greatpaw told about his plan to share stories. Nathaniel told about the chicken salad sandwiches and lemonade.

Nathaniel's parents shook their heads and said, "Don't get your hopes up, Nathaniel. There aren't many people Greatpaw's age around anymore."

At noon on Saturday Greatpaw and Nathaniel sat on the front porch, waiting for the crowd. Greatpaw made gallons of lemonade and stacks of chicken salad sandwiches. He planned to get the ice cream crank out later in the afternoon.

It turned out to be real lucky that Nathaniel liked lemonade and chicken salad sandwiches. . . .

After that day Greatpaw didn't feel much like telling stories anymore.

Nathaniel started bringing his dog, Johnson, with him to Greatpaw's house after school. "Johnson doesn't know any stories," Nathaniel told Greatpaw, "but he's a good listener."

Greatpaw tousled Nathaniel's hair, then Johnson's. But he didn't tell any stories.

Nathaniel invited Greatpaw to his third-grade class. "Twenty-five kids will know lots of stories to share with you," Nathaniel told Greatpaw on the way. "And then you can tell us yours."

But all the kids did was stare at Greatpaw's white hair, and all Greatpaw said was, "I used to have fiery red hair like Nathaniel's when I was a boy."

Nathaniel had almost given up on ever hearing Greatpaw's stories again, when one Sunday he saw a section in the newspaper that he'd never seen before.

On Monday Nathaniel paid a visit to the city editor's office. "I'd like to buy an ad," he said.

The next Sunday Nathaniel shuffled through the paper with his fingers crossed. Finally he reached the "CONFIDENTIALS," and read:

> 100-YEAR-OLD MAN—fiery, fit, and a fine
> storyteller—looking for 100-year-old
> friends—same. Call Nathaniel at 555-9007
> for interview.

All day Nathaniel waited by the phone with Johnson. At 6:13 P.M. the telephone rang.

"This is Sadie Johannsen," said a voice from the other end. "I'll be one hundred next April. I'm not quite as fiery and fit as I used to be, but I'm still a fine storyteller if I do say so myself."

An interview was arranged for the next evening in Nathaniel's kitchen.

"When I was a girl," Sadie
began, "my parents brought
me to America on a steamer
ship. We spent two weeks
tiltin' and turnin' on those
cold Atlantic waves." She
moved her hands in the air
to demonstrate.

"After we arrived," Sadie continued, "we lived in a tenement. It was so full of mice, you had to learn to dance. Quick steps and high, to keep the critters from crawlin' up your legs." She showed Nathaniel a few steps while still seated in her chair.

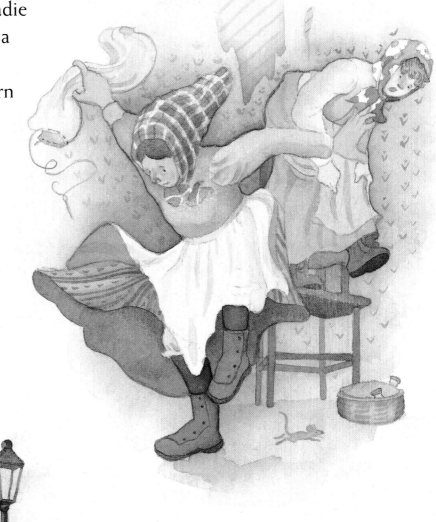

Then Sadie eyed three oranges in the fruit bowl. She scooped them up and started tossing them in the air. "I learned to juggle in the hopes the circus would hire me on. It came to the outskirts of our city every year. I never did join up, but I can still juggle when I set my mind to it."

Finally Sadie drew in a deep breath, leaned over her cane, and asked,
"Well, young man, how did I do? Did I pass?"

Nathaniel grinned. Johnson wagged his tail. "I'll be right back," Nathaniel told Sadie, running out the door.

He found Greatpaw whittling on the front porch.

"Greatpaw, I've been thinking, maybe you don't need lots of storytellers to share stories with you. Maybe just one would do."

And one *did* do just fine.

Every now and then, though, Sadie and Greatpaw like a slightly bigger audience. So the first of each month Nathaniel gathers his friends on Greatpaw and Sadie's front porch. While Sadie cranks the ice cream maker, Greatpaw makes chicken salad sandwiches and Nathaniel pours lemonade.

Sometimes Nathaniel and his friends tell stories of their own, but mostly they just listen.

After all,
Sadie and Greatpaw have had
a lot more time to practice.